Poppy and Max and the Snow Dog

For Daphne
SG

For Steve
LG

Reading Consultant: Prue Goodwin,
lecturer in education at the University of Reading

ORCHARD BOOKS
338 Euston Road, London NW1 3BH
Orchard Books Australia
Level 17/207 Kent Street, Sydney, NSW 2000

ISBN 978 1 84362 401 1 (hardback)
ISBN 978 1 84362 404 2 (paperback)

First published in hardback in by Orchard Books in 2007
First paperback publication in 2008

A CIP catalogue record for this book is available from the British Library.

1 3 5 7 9 10 8 6 4 2 (hardback)
1 3 5 7 9 10 8 6 4 2 (paperback)

Printed in China

Orchard Books is a division of Hachette Children's Books

www.orchardbooks.co.uk

Poppy and Max and the Snow Dog

Sally Grindley ⊶ Lindsey Gardiner

One cold morning, Poppy lay snuggled up in bed and thought, *I can't hear the birds singing.*

She prodded Max. "Stop snoring Max," she said. "I can't hear the birds singing."

Max lifted an ear. "That's because they are not singing," he grunted.

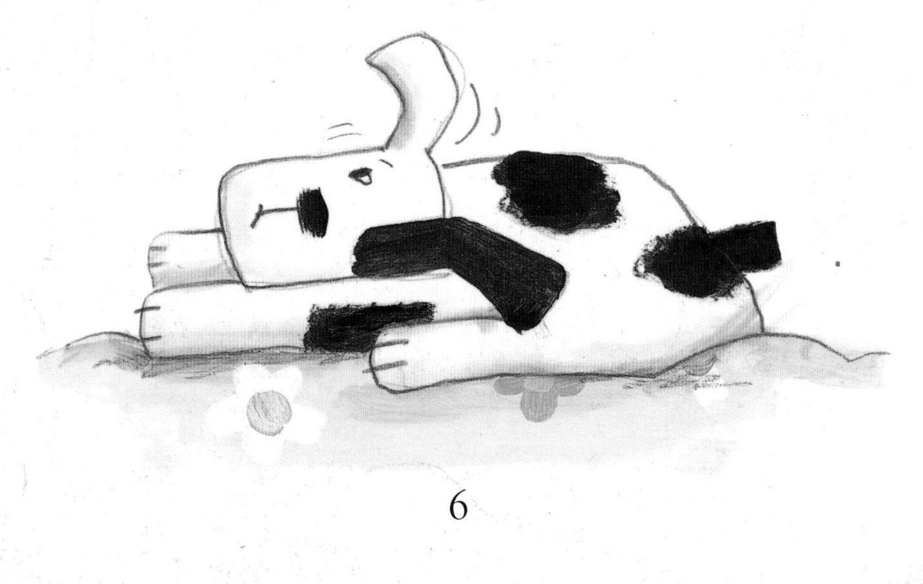

Poppy jumped out of bed and ran to the window.

"It's snowing, Max!" she squealed.

"I love it when everything is white and snowflakes are floating down from the sky."
"I love my bed," grunted Max.

“We can make a snowman, Max.
Come on, lazybones.”
“I am not a dog who likes getting cold,” grumbled Max.

“You’ll be warm in your scarf and hat,” said Poppy.

As soon as they had finished breakfast, they went out into the garden.
"Doesn't it look beautiful, Max?" cried Poppy.

"If you like that sort of thing," said Max. He pulled his hat down as low as it would go.
Poppy picked up a handful of snow and threw it in the air.

"Where shall we build our snowman?" she asked.
"Why does it have to be a snowman?" said Max. "Why not a snowdog?"

"Brilliant idea!" cried Poppy.
"Snowdog Max!"
"Yippee! Snowdog Max,"
cheered Max.

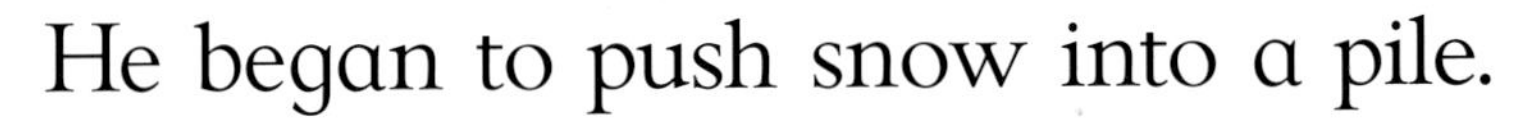

He began to push snow into a pile.

"Is Snowdog Max going to be sitting or standing?" asked Poppy.
"Standing," said Max. "Come on, Poppy, keep piling up the snow."

They pushed and patted and pushed and patted and the pile of snow began to grow.

"I'm getting hot," said Poppy.
"Me too," said Max, taking off his hat and scarf. "Don't stop, Poppy."

They pushed and patted and pushed and patted some more.

Max stepped back and looked at the snowdog's body. "It's big enough now, I think," he said. "It's a perfect body."

"Like yours!" said Poppy. "Shall we make the head now?"

"Of course," said Max.

They patted some snow into a ball,
then rolled it across the ground.
"Keep going, Poppy!" said Max.

The snowball grew bigger and bigger. "It's big enough now, I think," said Max. "Help me lift it on, Poppy."

When it was in place, they stepped back and looked at it.

"It's a perfect head," said Max.
"Like yours!" said Poppy. "Shall we do the face now?"

"I will have to be handsome," said Max.
"What shall we use for a nose?"
asked Poppy.
"Something dark," said Max.

He thought for a moment,
then ran indoors.

When Max came back he was
holding a chocolate muffin.
"This will be perfect," he said.
"Don't you want to eat it?"
chuckled Poppy.

"Snowdog Max can have it," said Max.
He pushed the muffin into the
snowball face.
"Brilliant," said Poppy.

"What about the eyes?" said Max.
Poppy ran indoors and came back
with two black buttons.

"Here are the eyes," she said.

"Now for the final touch," said Max. He put his hat on the snowdog's head, then he wrapped his scarf around its neck.

"There!" he said.

They stood back and looked at it.
"It doesn't look much like me," Max said sadly, after staring at it for a while. "It doesn't look much like a dog at all."

Suddenly, a head popped over the garden gate.
"What's that you have made?" said a voice.

"Hello, Billy," cried Poppy. "This is our . . ."

". . . Snow Thing," said Max quickly. "It's our Snow Thing, and it has stolen one of our muffins! Give it back," he growled.

He grabbed the muffin from the Snow Thing's face, and ran indoors.

Poppy looked at Billy. “I don’t suppose you have a spare muffin?”

Sally Grindley

Illustrated by Lindsey Gardiner

Poppy and Max and the Lost Puppy	978 1 84362 394 6	£4.99
Poppy and Max and the Snow Dog	978 1 84362 404 2	£4.99
Poppy and Max and the Fashion Show	978 1 84362 393 9	£4.99
Poppy and Max and the Sore Paw	978 1 84362 405 9	£4.99
Poppy and Max and the River Picnic	978 1 84362 395 3	£4.99
Poppy and Max and the Noisy Night	978 1 84362 409 7	£4.99
Poppy and Max and the Big Wave	978 1 84362 519 3	£4.99
Poppy and Max and Too Many Muffins	978 1 84362 410 3	£4.99